LOVE ON THE RUN

BHUSHAN PATIL

Made with ♥ on the Notion Press Platform
www.notionpress.com

"To all the couples who have found their happily ever after, and to all the people who believe in the power of love. This story is for you. May your love continue to inspire and guide you through all of life's challenges."

Contents

Foreword

In a world filled with uncertainty and change, it is easy to lose sight of what truly matters. But as I read the story of Lily and Jack, I was reminded of the enduring power of love.

Their journey, from their first meeting on the campaign trail to their final days together, is a testament to the strength of the human spirit and the resilience of the human heart.

Their love for each other sustained them through every challenge and obstacle, and it ultimately brought them the happily ever after that they deserved.

I hope that their story will inspire you, as it did me, to believe in the power of love and to chase your own happily ever after.

Preface

When I first met Lily and Jack(name for this story), I knew that they were something special. Their love for each other was palpable, and it was clear that they were meant to be together.

As I followed their journey, from their first meeting on the campaign trail to their final days together, I was struck by the depth of their love and their commitment to each other.

Through every challenge and obstacle, Lily and Jack stuck together and supported each other, and their love only grew stronger.

Their story is a testament to the enduring power of love, and it is a reminder that with love, anything is possible.

I hope that their story will inspire you, as it did me, to believe in the power of love and to chase your own happily ever after.

Acknowledgements

I would like to express my heartfelt gratitude to all the people who have supported me throughout the writing of this novel.

To my family, who have always believed in me and encouraged me to follow my dreams, thank you. Your love and support have meant the world to me.

To my editor, who helped me shape and refine this story, thank you. Your guidance and insight were invaluable.

And to my readers, thank you for taking the time to read this story. I hope that it has touched your heart and inspired you to believe in the power of love.

Finally, a special thank you to Lily and Jack(names for this story), whose love and determination inspired this novel. Their legacy lives on in these pages, and I am grateful to have had the opportunity to tell their story.

Prologue

As I sit on the porch of my house, looking out at the sunset, I can't help but reflect on the journey that brought me here.

It all started on the campaign trail, where I met the love of my life. From the moment we locked eyes, I knew that our paths were meant to intersect.

We knew that we had to fight for our love, as the world seemed determined to keep us apart. But we never gave up, and we always stuck together.

Through every challenge and obstacle, we supported each other and believed in the power of our love. And in the end, it was that love that sustained us and brought us the happily ever after that we deserved.

As I close my eyes for the final time, I know that I have lived a full and rewarding life. I have accomplished a lot, and I have made a difference in the world.

But most importantly, I have found my happily ever after. I have found love, and I have found my place in the world.

And I know that I have done it all with the love of my life by my side.

This is our story.(This story is purely authors imagination and not related to anyone to the best of my knowledge)

1

The Assignment

Lily sat at her desk, staring at the blinking cursor on her computer screen. She had been trying to write the opening paragraph of her latest article for the past hour, but the words just weren't coming.

"Come on, Lily," she muttered to herself, "you can do this."

She took a deep breath and began to type:

"The race for the White House is heating up, and this year's election is shaping up to be one of the most contentious in recent memory. With a crowded field of candidates vying for the nomination, it's anyone's guess who will come out on top. But one thing is certain: it's going to be a long and grueling campaign season."

Lily leaned back in her chair and reread the paragraph. It was solid, if a bit uninspired. She needed something more to hook the reader's attention. She thought for a moment, then added:

"And at the center of it all is Jack Thompson, the charming and charismatic senator from New York who has emerged as the frontrunner for the Democratic nomination. His campaign has been shrouded in secrecy, but as the only journalist granted access to his inner circle,

I'm about to get an inside look at the man behind the campaign."

Lily smiled to herself. That was more like it. She saved the document and stood up, stretching her arms above her head. She was just about to head out for a much-needed coffee break when her editor, Janine, appeared in the doorway.

"Lily, can I see you in my office?" Janine asked, her voice laced with excitement.

Lily's heart skipped a beat. This was it – the moment she had been waiting for. She grabbed her notebook and followed Janine down the hall to her office.

"Close the door behind you," Janine said as they entered. Lily did as she was told, her heart pounding in her chest.

"Sit down, Lily," Janine said, gesturing to the chair in front of her desk. Lily sat, trying to steady her breathing.

"I have a big assignment for you," Janine said, a broad smile on her face. "I want you to cover Jack Thompson's campaign for the duration of the primary season. You'll have full access to his team and his events, and I want you to give our readers an inside look at the man and his campaign. What do you say?"

Lily couldn't believe it. This was the opportunity of a lifetime – the chance to cover one of the biggest political campaigns in history. And to top it off, she would be getting an up-close look at the charming and charismatic Jack Thompson. She couldn't wait to see what the campaign had in store.

"I'm in," she said, grinning from ear to ear.

"I knew you wouldn't disappoint me," Janine said, clapping Lily on the back. "You leave for New York tomorrow. Pack your bags and get ready to hit the campaign trail."

As Lily left Janine's office, she couldn't help but feel a mix of excitement and nervousness. She had a feeling that this assignment was going to be the ride of her life.

Lily spent the rest of the day packing and making arrangements for her extended stay on the campaign trail. She couldn't believe that she was actually going to be following Jack Thompson around the country as he campaigned for the presidency. It was a dream come true for any journalist, and Lily was determined to make the most of it.

She arrived in New York the next day and was met at the airport by a member of Jack's campaign team. From there, she was whisked away to the campaign headquarters, where she was introduced to the rest of the team and given a tour of the facilities.

She was struck by how professional and organized everything was. The headquarters was bustling with activity, with staffers rushing back and forth and phones ringing off the hook. Lily couldn't believe that she was actually going to be a part of all of this.

As the day went on, she began to get a sense of the campaign's strategy and how it was being run. She also got a chance to meet Jack in person for the first time, and she was immediately struck by his charisma and charm. He was even more handsome and charming in person than he was on TV, and Lily couldn't help but feel a little bit starstruck.

Despite the frenetic pace of the campaign, Lily found herself falling into a routine over the next few weeks. She spent her days attending events, following Jack around the country, and writing articles about his campaign. And as she got to know him better, she found herself drawn to him in a way she couldn't quite explain.

But Lily knew that a relationship with Jack was out of the question. He was the candidate, and she was the journalist. It was a conflict of interest that could ruin both of their careers.

As the primary season wore on, Lily and Jack found themselves spending more and more time together, and their feelings for each other grew stronger by the day. But with the election looming and the media watching their every move, they knew they had to keep their relationship a secret.

As the stakes got higher and the pressure mounted, Lily and Jack were forced to make a choice: their love or their careers. How far were they willing to go to be together, and would their love survive the glare of the public eye?

2

On the Campaign Trail

Lily and Jack spent the next few months crisscrossing the country, attending events and rallies and meeting with voters. The campaign was grueling, with long days and late nights, but Lily didn't mind. She was having the time of her life, and getting to see Jack in action was a thrill like no other.

As she watched him speak to crowds of supporters, she couldn't help but be impressed by his passion and conviction. He was a natural politician, with a way of connecting with people that was both sincere and effortless. And as she got to know him better, she came to appreciate his intelligence and his sense of humor. He was unlike any man she had ever met, and she found herself falling for him more and more each day.

But their relationship was still a secret, and Lily knew that they had to be careful. The media was constantly watching them, and a single slip-up could ruin everything. They had to be discreet and keep their distance when they were in public, even though all they wanted to do was be together.

As the primary season wore on, Lily and Jack found themselves spending more and more time alone together. They would sneak away from the campaign trail whenever they could, stealing moments of privacy and intimacy whenever they could. And as they grew closer, Lily began to wonder if they could ever be together for real.

But with the election looming and the pressure mounting, Lily knew that she had to make a choice. She couldn't keep living in secret forever. She had to decide whether she was willing to risk everything for love, or if she would have to let Jack go.

3

The Decision

As the primary season drew to a close, Lily found herself at a crossroads. She had fallen for Jack deeply and couldn't imagine life without him, but she also knew that their relationship was forbidden. She was a journalist, and he was a candidate. It was a conflict of interest that could ruin both of their careers.

She tried to push the thoughts to the back of her mind and focus on the campaign, but it was becoming increasingly difficult. Every time she saw Jack, she felt her heart swell with love and longing. She knew that she had to make a decision, and soon.

One night, after a long day on the campaign trail, Lily found herself alone in her hotel room, staring at the ceiling and wondering what to do. She knew that she couldn't keep living in secrecy forever, but she was also terrified of the consequences of coming clean.

Just as she was about to fall asleep, her phone rang. It was Jack.

"Lily, I need to see you," he said, his voice urgent. "Can you meet me in the lobby in ten minutes?"

Lily hesitated for a moment, then threw off the covers and got out of bed. She knew that this was it – the moment of truth. She had to make a choice.

She met Jack in the lobby a few minutes later, and he led her outside to a quiet spot where they could talk.

"Lily, I can't take this anymore," he said, pacing back and forth. "I love you, and I can't keep pretending that I don't. We have to make a decision – are we going to be together, or are we going to let our careers come between us?"

Lily took a deep breath and looked into Jack's eyes. She knew what she wanted, and she knew what she had to do.

"I love you, Jack," she said, her voice shaking. "And I don't want to let anything come between us. I don't care about my career or what anyone else thinks. I just want to be with you."

Jack took her hand and squeezed it tightly.

"I feel the same way, Lily," he said, his eyes shining with tears. "I love you, and I want to be with you. Let's do this – let's be together, no matter what."

Lily threw her arms around Jack and hugged him tightly. She knew that this was the start of something new, something beautiful and fragile and precious. And she knew that no matter what the future held, she was ready to face it with Jack by her side.

4

The Fallouts

Lily and Jack knew that their love was unconventional and forbidden, as they were working for competing campaigns. But they couldn't resist the pull that they felt towards each other.

They tried to keep their relationship a secret, but it was only a matter of time before the media caught on. And as their love became the focus of the campaign, they knew that they had to face the fallouts of their relationship.

They faced criticism and backlash from both campaigns, and they knew that they had to make a choice. They could either give in to the pressure and end their relationship, or they could fight for their love and make it work.

They knew that it wouldn't be easy, but they were determined to make it work. They knew that they had found something special, and they were willing to fight for it.

But as they navigated the fallouts of their relationship, they knew that they had to be stronger than ever. They had to stand up for their love and for each other, and they had to be willing to fight for what they believed in.

And as they walked hand in hand down the campaign trail, they knew that they had found their happily ever after. They had found love, and they were determined to make it work, no matter what.

As the campaign heated up, Lily and Jack faced more and more challenges. They knew that they had to be careful about how they presented their relationship to the public, as they didn't want to jeopardize the campaigns that they were working for.

But as the media spotlight intensified, they knew that they had to stand up for their love. They knew that they had found something special, and they were determined to make it work, no matter what.

As they faced the fallouts of their relationship, they knew that they had to be stronger than ever. They had to stand up for their love and for each other, and they had to be willing to fight for what they believed in.

And in the end, it was their love and determination that helped them weather the storm. They knew that they had each other's back, no matter what, and they were ready to face whatever the future held.

As they walked hand in hand down the campaign trail, they knew that they had found their happily ever after. They had found love, and they were determined to make it work, no matter what.

And as they looked into each other's eyes, they knew that they had found their happily ever after. They had found love, and they were ready to face whatever the future held, as long as they had each other by their side.

5
The New Normal

Lily and Jack knew that their relationship would not be easy, but they were determined to make it work. They were in love, and they were willing to fight for each other no matter what.

The first few weeks were tough, as they adjusted to their new normal. Lily was no longer covering the campaign, and Jack was under intense scrutiny from the media and his political rivals. But they stuck together, supporting each other through the tough times and celebrating the small victories.

As the election drew near, Jack's campaign faced a series of challenges and setbacks. But through it all, he remained focused and determined, with Lily by his side every step of the way.

And in the end, it all paid off. On election night, Jack was declared the winner, and he and Lily were surrounded by cheers and tears as they celebrated their victory.

As they stood on the stage, holding hands and looking out at the sea of faces, Lily knew that this was just the beginning. They had a long road ahead of them, with many challenges and obstacles to overcome. But she was ready for it, as long as she had Jack by her side.

As they walked off the stage and into the night, Lily knew that she had made the right decision. She had chosen love over career, and she had no regrets. She was ready to face whatever the future held, as long as she had Jack by her side.

Lily and Jack held hands as they walked off the stage and into the night, surrounded by cheers and tears. They had done it – they had won the election and were about to embark on the next chapter of their lives.

But they knew that the road ahead would not be easy. They were going to face many challenges and obstacles as they navigated their new roles, and they were going to have to work hard to maintain their relationship in the glare of the public eye.

But they were ready for it. They were in love, and they were willing to fight for each other no matter what.

As they walked through the crowd, smiling and shaking hands, Lily couldn't help but feel a sense of pride and accomplishment. She had made it through the campaign season and had come out on top. She had also found love in the process, and she was grateful for that.

As they made their way back to their hotel room, Lily knew that she had made the right decision. She had chosen love over career, and she had no regrets. She was ready to face whatever the future held, as long as she had Jack by her side.

They walked into their room and collapsed onto the bed, laughing and crying and holding each other tight. They had done it – they had won the election and had come through the other side.

They lay there for a long time, holding each other and basking in the glow of their victory. They knew that this was just the beginning, and that they had a long road ahead of them. But they were ready for it, as long as they had each other.

And as they fell asleep in each other's arms, Lily knew that she had found her happily ever after.

6

The Inauguration

The next few months were a blur of activity as Lily and Jack prepared for Jack's inauguration as President of the United States. There were endless meetings and events, and Lily was constantly on the go, trying to keep up with everything.

But despite the hectic pace, she was having the time of her life. She was living in the White House, working as Jack's chief of staff, and getting to see him in action every day. She was also getting to know the rest of the staff and making new friends.

And as the inauguration day approached, Lily couldn't help but feel a sense of excitement and pride. She knew that this was a once-in-a-lifetime opportunity, and she was determined to make the most of it.

On the day of the inauguration, Lily stood by Jack's side as he took the oath of office and delivered his inaugural address. She watched with tears in her eyes as he spoke about hope and unity and the promise of a brighter future.

And as he finished his speech and the crowd erupted in cheers, Lily knew that this was the beginning of a new era. She was proud to be a part of it, and she was determined to make a difference.

As they walked off the stage, hand in hand, Lily knew that she had found her place in the world. She was no longer just a journalist – she was a leader, and a partner, and a friend. She had found her calling, and she was ready to make the most of it.

As Lily and Jack walked off the stage, hand in hand, they were surrounded by cheers and applause. They had just taken their first steps as President and First Lady of the United States, and they were ready for the challenge.

They spent the next few months settling into their new roles and getting to know the staff and the White House. It was a busy and hectic time, but they were having the time of their lives. They were working together to make a difference, and they were making a real impact.

As the months went by, Lily and Jack grew closer and stronger. They were a team, and they were in this together. They faced challenges and setbacks, but they always stuck together and supported each other.

And as the years went by, they watched each other grow and change, and they were proud of each other's achievements. They knew that they had each other's back, no matter what.

In the end, Lily and Jack's love for each other was the driving force behind everything they did. They were partners, and friends, and lovers, and they knew that they were meant to be together.

As they stood on the White House lawn, looking out at the world, they knew that they had come a long way from that first meeting on the campaign trail. They had faced challenges and obstacles, but they had always stuck together, and they had come out on top.

They knew that the road ahead would not be easy, but they were ready for it. They had each other, and they had love, and that was all they needed. They were ready to face whatever the future held, as long as they had each other by their side.

7
The First Lady

As Lily settled into her role as First Lady, she found herself faced with a whole new set of challenges. She was no longer just Jack's partner – she was a public figure in her own right, and she had to navigate the complex world of politics and diplomacy.

But she was up for the challenge. She had always been a strong and independent woman, and she was determined to make a difference. She focused on issues that mattered to her, such as education and healthcare, and she worked tirelessly to promote her causes.

As the years went by, Lily became a respected and influential figure in her own right. She was admired for her intelligence, her compassion, and her dedication to making the world a better place.

But she never forgot her roots. She always made time for the people who mattered most to her – her family, her friends, and Jack. She knew that they were the ones who had supported her every step of the way, and she was grateful for them.

As she stood on the White House lawn, looking out at the world, Lily knew that she had come a long way. She had faced challenges and obstacles, but she had always stuck to her principles and remained true to herself.

And as she looked at Jack, standing by her side, she knew that she had found her happily ever after. They had come through it all together, and they were stronger and happier than ever.

As they walked into the sunset, hand in hand, Lily knew that she had found her place in the world. She was a leader, a partner, and a friend, and she was ready to face whatever the future held.

As the years went by, Lily and Jack continued to work together to make a difference in the world. They faced challenges and setbacks, but they always stuck together and supported each other.

And as they approached the end of Jack's second term, they knew that it was time to start thinking about the future. They had accomplished a lot during their time in the White House, but they both knew that there was still more work to be done.

They spent the next few months considering their options and weighing their choices. They talked to their advisors and their friends, and they listened to the advice of the people they trusted.

In the end, they made their decision. They were going to run for a third term, and they were going to do it together.

They knew that it would be a tough campaign, but they were ready for it. They had each other, and they had love, and that was all they needed.

As they stood on the White House lawn, announcing their decision to the world, Lily knew that this was the right choice. She was ready to continue the work that they had started, and she was ready to face whatever the future held.

As the campaign season got underway, Lily and Jack threw themselves into the race with all of their energy and enthusiasm. They traveled the country, meeting with voters and talking about their vision for the future.

And in the end, they came out on top. They won the election, and they were re-elected as President and First Lady of the United States.

As they stood on the stage, holding hands and looking out at the sea of faces, Lily knew that this was just the beginning. They had a long road ahead of them, with many challenges and obstacles to overcome. But she was ready for it, as long as she had Jack by her side.

As they walked off the stage and into the night, Lily knew that she had found her happily ever after. She had found love, and she had found her place in the world. And she was ready to face whatever the future held, as long as she had Jack by her side.

8
The Final Term

As Lily and Jack began their final term in the White House, they knew that they had a lot of work to do. They had big plans for their final years in office, and they were determined to make the most of them.

They focused on issues that mattered to them, such as education, healthcare, and the environment, and they worked tirelessly to promote their causes. They traveled the country, meeting with voters and talking about their vision for the future.

And as the years went by, they watched each other grow and change, and they were proud of each other's achievements. They knew that they had each other's back, no matter what.

As the end of their term approached, Lily and Jack knew that it was time to start thinking about the future. They had accomplished a lot during their time in the White House, but they both knew that there was still more work to be done.

They spent the next few months considering their options and weighing their choices. They talked to their advisors and their friends, and they listened to the advice of the people they trusted.

In the end, they made their decision. They were going to retire from politics, and they were going to do it together.

They knew that it would be a tough decision, but they were ready for it. They had each other, and they had love, and that was all they needed.

As they stood on the White House lawn, announcing their decision to the world, Lily knew that this was the right choice. She was ready to start the next chapter of her life, and she was ready to face whatever the future held.

As they walked off the stage and into the sunset, hand in hand, Lily knew that she had found her happily ever after. She had found love, and she had found her place in the world. And she was ready to face whatever the future held, as long as she had Jack by her side.

As Lily and Jack left the White House and retired from politics, they knew that they had a lot of adjusting to do. They had spent the past eight years living in the public eye, and they were looking forward to some privacy and solitude.

They bought a beautiful house in a quiet neighborhood, and they spent the next few months settling in and getting to know their new community. They made new friends, and they enjoyed the simple pleasures of life – cooking, gardening, and spending time with each other.

But they didn't completely disconnect from the world. They stayed active in their causes, and they traveled the country, giving talks and raising awareness for the issues that mattered most to them.

And as the years went by, they watched each other grow and change, and they were proud of each other's achievements. They knew that they had each other's back, no matter what.

As they approached their golden years, Lily and Jack knew that they had come a long way from their first meeting on the campaign trail. They had faced challenges and obstacles, but they had always stuck together, and they had come out on top.

They knew that the road ahead would not be easy, but they were ready for it. They had each other, and they had love, and that was all they needed.

As they sat on the porch of their house, looking out at the sunset, Lily knew that she had found her happily ever after. She had found love, and she had found her place in the world. And she was ready to face whatever the future held, as long as she had Jack by her side.

9

The Climax

Lily and Jack had always known that their love was strong, but they never expected it to be put to the ultimate test.

As they approached the end of their lives, they knew that they had lived full and rewarding lives. They had accomplished a lot, and they had made a difference in the world.

But they also knew that they were not done yet. They had a lot of living left to do, and they were determined to make the most of it.

They continued to travel and explore new places, and they made a point of staying active and engaged in the world around them. They knew that they had a lot to offer, and they were determined to make a difference.

As the years went by, Lily and Jack watched each other grow and change, and they were proud of each other's achievements. They knew that they had each other's back, no matter what.

But when Jack was diagnosed with a terminal illness, everything changed. Lily knew that she had to do everything in her power to save him.

She searched for every possible treatment and cure, and she never gave up hope. She knew that she could not imagine a life without Jack, and she was determined to do whatever it took to save him.

As Jack's health declined, Lily refused to give up. She stayed by his side, holding his hand and offering him comfort and support. She knew that she could not lose him, and she was determined to fight for him.

And in the end, it was Lily's love and determination that saved Jack. Against all odds, Jack made a miraculous recovery, and he knew that it was all thanks to Lily. He knew that he could not have made it through without her, and he was grateful for every moment that they had together.

As they sat on the porch of their house, looking out at the sunset, Lily knew that she had found her happily ever after. She had found love, and she had found her place in the world. And she was ready to face whatever the future held, as long as she had Jack by her side.

They looked back on their journey together, and they knew that they had built a life that was full of love, and they were grateful for every moment.

They had come a long way from their first meeting on the campaign trail. They had faced challenges and obstacles, but they had always stuck together, and they had come out on top.

They had built a life that was full of love, and they were grateful for every moment.

As the sun set on their golden years, Lily and Jack knew that they had found their happily ever after. And they were ready to face whatever the future held, as long as they had each other by their side.

And as they took their final breaths, They had found love, and they had found their place in the world.

"end matter: A Look Behind The Scenes"

About the Author:

Bhushan Patil

Acknowledgments:

I would like to express my heartfelt gratitude to all the people who have supported me throughout the writing of this novel.

To my family, who have always believed in me and encouraged me to follow my dreams, thank you. Your love and support have meant the world to me.

To my editor, who helped me shape and refine this story, thank you. Your guidance and insight were invaluable.

And to my readers, thank you for taking the time to read this story. I hope that it has touched your heart and inspired you to believe in the power of love.

Finally, a special thank you to Lily and Jack, whose love and determination inspired this novel. Their legacy lives on in these pages, and I am grateful to have had the opportunity to tell their story.

Other Books by the Author:

"The Practical Path To Prosperity"

Connect with the Author:

Instagram:- @itzbhushanpatil